The Barber of Bingo

For Peter, Ellen, and Emma.

*Many thanks to Jake Morrissey
for his support and insight during
the creation of this book.*

The Barber of Bingo

written by
Beth Ruediger

illustrated by
John McPherson
and
Laura McPherson

ANDREWS AND McMEEL
A Universal Press Syndicate Company
Kansas City

ISBN: 0-8362-2690-9

Library of Congress Catalog Card Number: 96-85638

ATTENTION SCHOOLS AND BUSINESSES

Andrews and McMeel books are available at quantity discounts with bulk purchase for educational, business, or sales promotional use. For information, please write to: Special Sales Department, Andrews and McMeel, 4520 Main Street, Kansas City, Missouri 64111.

Mr. Vic was a barber in the town of Bingo. He had a tidy little shop across from the town park. Everyone loved the way he cut hair.

5

Mr. Vic clipped feathers or fur. He snipped tails and whiskers. He shampooed and dried animals of all sizes. He had one assistant, Charlie, a chipmunk, and a team of helper mice who kept the shop as clean as a cat's paw. On Saturday mornings they trimmed claws and shined hoofs, four for a nickel.

There was just one thing Mr. Vic would not do. "I will not have bears in my shop!" he would say. "They have fleas. They push and shove and drink shampoo. I have even heard they tell ridiculous jokes." He had a sign on the wall that read, "NO BEARS AT ALL!"

One morning an odd thing happened. A woman in a yellow dress poked her head into the shop. "Knock, knock!" she called.

Mr. Vic looked up from his work. "Who's there?" Mr. Vic had never seen her before, but she looked very much like a bear.

"I'm Polly," the woman said. She smiled and clambered into a barber chair. "I'd like a cut, please, but leave it long around the ears."

Mr. Vic glanced at Charlie and fluttered his tail nervously on the floor. He coughed and placed a paw on the "NO BEARS AT ALL!" sign. The woman didn't seem to notice. "Pardon me, ma'am," he said, "but are you a bear?" The woman, however, was peering at herself in the mirror and did not answer.

Mr. Vic sighed. Maybe she wasn't really a bear. And if she was, perhaps she wouldn't tell her relatives she'd been to his shop. The last thing he wanted was a batch of bears showing up, expecting hair cuts. He trimmed her hair and watched her leave, chewing her paws and grinning.

The next day she was back, this time with a tall, older bear. The shop was busy, and they sat down to wait. Mr. Vic frowned at them as he worked, hoping they would leave. But they sat quietly talking. Finally Mr. Vic called them up and trimmed the old bear's shaggy snout.

11

Mr. Vic was very grumpy after they left. He grumbled as he dusted the snout fur from his shoulders. "A snout trim today! What will it be tomorrow?"

An owl flapped up onto the barber chair. "I found them both quite interesting. Why haven't I seen them here before?"

"Hmmph," said Mr. Vic.

Two days later Polly was back. This time she had five cubs with her. They sat still as stones while Mr. Vic buzzed their heads.

"What sweet children," remarked a deer.

Mr. Vic said nothing, but he gave each cub a lollipop as it left.

The next day an awful surprise was waiting for Mr. Vic when he got
to his shop. Bears and bears and bears. Circling and snuffling outside

14 his door.

At the front of the crowd was Polly. "I brought a few friends," she
hollered when Mr. Vic peeked out the window.

"Yikes!" Mr. Vic clutched his whiskers. "What should we do, Charlie?" He tried to hide, but the bears had already spied him.

16   At opening time they streamed into his shop.

They filled the chairs and lined the walls. They perched on the
counters and the drinking fountain chanting, "HAIR CUT! HAIR CUT!"

Mr. Vic stared at the mob of furry heads until the room fell silent. He gazed at row after row of bright, round eyes. The bears all blinked back at him with quiet smiles. Finally he lifted his scissors and began to cut.

As he worked he kept a close watch for fleas, but he didn't see even one. The bears sipped orange soda instead of shampoo and waited patiently for their turns.

It was true they told ridiculous jokes. They had a group of sheep silly with giggles. But the jokes were very funny. When Polly led the whole crowd in a sing-along, Mr. Vic kept time with his tail. And each bear that left the shop gave him a furry hug.

The place was a ruin, though, by closing time. Fur was heaped on
20   the floor right up to Mr. Vic's teeth.

It stuck to the walls and floated through the air so thickly there was no room even to sneeze. Charlie was whimpering, and some of the mice were missing.

Mr. Vic squinted sadly through the furry gloom. "Rats, Charlie," he said. "This place is a mess. But, you know, I really liked those bears. They're not scary at all. They're good folks. Did you hear the one about the chicken crossing the road?" He waded through the fur until he reached the "NO BEARS AT ALL!" sign. He yanked it down and chewed 22 it to bits. "Now I must think hard about all of this," he said.

He had been wrong about the bears.
Now he wanted to make them welcome in his shop. But what could he
do about all the fur? None of his old customers could even get in the
door. They walked past and said, "Poor Mr. Vic."

He sat and thought for a week. He and Charlie tried to shovel the
fur out the windows. But it had settled into a pile as thick and slippery
as a haystack and heavy as a hill. It would not budge.

23

Then one night as he sat thinking, there was a soft knock at the door. Polly the bear wedged her fuzzy snout into the shop. "Psst ... Mr. Vic. Bear fur makes fabulous clothing. Did you know?" She tossed him a fat catalog. "Let me know if I can help you." She waved good-bye.

NO GRUNTING OR HOWLING, PLEASE!

H
• SMA (M
• LAF (GO.
• BUF
• HO

TUESD TAIL TRIMMIN ONLY 5

L.L.BEAR
THE EVERYTHING CATALOG!

Mr. Vic pawed through the catalog until he was filled with ideas. In the morning he hung a sign outside his shop that said, "Closed for Repairs." He passed out fliers that read, "Come to the Grand Opening of the Salon de Bingo Extraordinaire in Two Weeks." He ordered several new things from the catalog. Then he and Charlie got to work.

First they built a new room onto the barbershop. Then they
hammered together a large odd-looking contraption that Mr. Vic
named the Bear Fur Scooper-Mover Machine. By the time it was all
hooked up, a truck had arrived with seven big boxes. Mr. Vic unpacked
them and assembled a shiny fur molding machine at one end of the

new room. Near the window he put a row of shelves and racks for clothes. He showed the mice how to use the fur molder. Charlie practiced driving the Scooper-Mover. Then Mr. Vic clapped his tail. "Ready, set, go!" he shouted.

27

The Scooper-Mover
lurched forward and
grabbed the first bite
of fur. The mice washed and
dried it and stuffed it into
the molding machine.

In exactly four minutes the door popped open and out slid a
beautiful fur wedding gown.

"Holy mackerel, look at that!" Mr. Vic shouted. "It works! Keep it

coming, team."

Slowly, what had once been used fur became lovely clothing. Fur coats and caps, dresses and jeans, socks and swim suits soon filled the shelves of the Salon de Bingo Extraordinaire.

Mr. Vic gave his helpers one week to work. Then he was ready for the grand opening. He hired Polly to run the new store. A band played and refreshments were served.

People poured into the salon to see the exciting new fur clothing. Fur coats were sold out in the first hour.

Mr. Vic's barbershop was ready to go again. There was an extra chair and barber for busy days. And a new sign on the wall read, "EVERYONE WELCOME HERE!"